To my two amazing kids—Alex and Morgan. You are my inspiration.

And to Scott, your love and support mean the world to me.

Special thanks to Dyan Smith Chandler, Taylor Tomasini and Theresa Tomasini

Alex's Ten-Dollar Adventure
Published by:
Three Bean Press, LLC
P.O. Box 301711
Jamaica Plain, MA 02130
info@threebeanpress.com • www.threebeanpress.com

Publishers Cataloging-in-Publication Data
Bailey, Wendy
Alex's Ten-Dollar Adventure / by Wendy Bailey.
p. cm.
Summary: When Alex receives money for his birthday, he heads off to buy a coveted action figure. But with stops along the way for ice cream and lemonade, can Alex afford the toy by the time he reaches the store? Kids get to learn about saving for a sunny day along with this lovable little boy.

ISBN 978-0-9903315-0-6
[1. Children—Fiction. 2. Young Readers—Fiction. 3. Money—Fiction. 4. Saving—Fiction.
5. Math—Fiction. 6. Earning—Fiction. 7. Spending—Fiction.] I. D'Elia, Ernie, Ill. II. Title.
LCCN 2014938549

Printed and bound in Guangzhou, China, by Everbest Printing Company, Ltd., through Four Colour Print Group in June 2014. Batch 116920.2

10 9 8 7 6 5 4 3 2 1

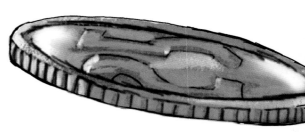

Alex'$
TEN-DOLLAR
Adventure

Written by Wendy Bailey

Illustrated by Ernie D'Elia

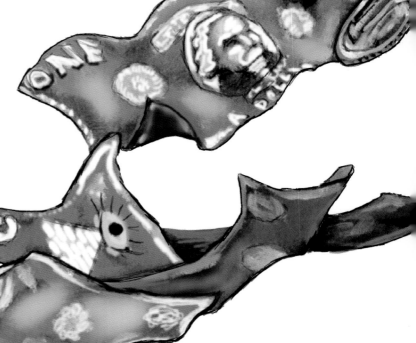

Alex's birthday was coming, and he was excited!
He was having a party. His friends were invited.
The mail truck pulled up while he was having a snack.
There was a letter for him at the top of the stack.

"Look, Mom," called Alex. "I got mail today!"
"A birthday card!" said Mom. "What does it say?"
"It says, *Happy 8th Birthday to a real champ!*
Have a super day!
Love, Grandma and Gramps"

"There's money inside!" said Alex. "Yippee!"

"One, two, three, four...five dollars for me!
I've got five dollars, Mom! Isn't that cool?
I bet I'm the richest kid in my school."

"Five dollars!" said Mom.
"You're one lucky boy."
"What can five dollars buy?"
he asked, jumping for joy.

"Can it buy a new scooter
or a new baseball bat?

Can it buy a new bike or
something like that?"

"Five dollars," said Mom,
"isn't enough for a bike.
But I'm sure you could find
something else that you'd like."
"Or," said Mom, "you could
save your money instead.
Why, isn't your piggy bank
under your bed?"

"Are you sure about this?" asked Mom with a frown,
as he took out his bank and turned it upside down.
Out came a dollar, then another and two more,
then two quarters and five dimes fell onto the floor.

Alex counted and said, "Four more dollars for me.
Plus two quarters and five dimes each make fifty cents, see?
Fifty plus fifty equals one dollar more,
Which, added to four, gives me five more for the store!"

$$5.00$$
$$+ 4.00$$
$$= 9.00$$
$$+ .50$$
$$= 9.50$$
$$+ .50$$
$$= 10.00$$

"With ten dollars I'll have enough money to buy
that awesome new action hero called 'Rocket Guy.'
Rocket Guy is so cool. He is two toys in one!
A superhero plus a rocket makes for hours of fun."

"Alex, dear," said Mom,
"Do you have to spend it all?"

"It won't cost that much, Mom.
Rocket Guy's small!"

"I'll take my nine dollars, two quarters, five dimes.
Please, Mom, can I go? I'll be home in no time!"

The sun shined bright as Alex biked to the shop,
but his legs grew tired and he wanted to stop.
It's so hot, thought Alex, when he heard
someone call,

"Get your ice-cold
lemonade here!
Size large or size small!"

Lemonade, thought Alex, *Now that's what I'd like.*
And he stopped at the curb and hopped off his bike.
Help Send Me to Camp, read the sign at the stand,
and a girl with red hair held a pitcher in hand.

"I'm raising money for camp," said the girl with a smile.
"Will you buy a drink, please? I've been here quite a while."
"Sure," answered Alex, "I'll take the smallest you've got.
I'm off to the toy store, so I can't spend a lot."

"That's fifty cents, please," said the girl as she poured.
"Since it's such a hot day, I'll fill yours a bit more."

Alex paid her two quarters and said, "Thanks for the drink,"
then sat down with his lemonade and started to think.

If I subtract that fifty cents,
Alex thought as he sipped,
that leaves me nine
dollars and fifty cents
for my trip.

"Thanks again," said Alex as
he drank the last drop.
"Thank you," said the girl.
"I am sure glad you stopped."

MORGAN's
LEMONADE
STAND

10.00
− .50

$ 9.50

Alex hopped back on his bike and pedaled up the street.
Ahead was a shop that sold ice cream and sweets.
Ice cream, he thought, *is the greatest food in the world.*
The best flavors are chocolate and vanilla—swirled!

Alex stopped his bike, thinking,
It's so hot today.
I'll just get a small cone and then
be on my way.
It cost him one dollar
and twenty cents for his treat,
plus ten cents for sprinkles.
Then he dove in to eat.

"Yummy!" said Alex.
"This ice cream tastes
really great!"

He subtracted,
"Nine dollars minus one
equals eight.

Fifty cents minus thirty leaves
two dimes I might need.
So I'll ride to the
toy store at Rocket
Guy speed!"

Alex scarfed down the ice cream without even a drip,
then he spotted the toy store—the point of his trip.
The colorful shop brimmed with aisles of toys,
like pretty dolls for girls and action heroes for boys.

Alex found Rocket Guy near the
remote-control cars,
in a rectangular box with
red, white and blue stars.
Nine dollars and ninety-nine cents
was the price.
Alex couldn't believe it;
he read the tag twice.

"I had ten dollars!
Now I only have eight!

I should have saved my money.
Now it's too late.
My two dimes won't help.
Oh, this is a mess!
I really thought Rocket Guy
would have cost less."

What do I do? thought Alex.
I need my mom!
When things don't go well,
she always stays calm.
I could buy something else,
but it won't be as good.
So Alex rode his bike home
as fast as he could.

When he got there, his mom asked,

"Where's Rocket Guy?"
"I didn't buy him," said Alex.
"Want to know why?"

"Do you want to tell me? If not, that's okay.
I'm just glad that you're back. It's such a hot day."

Moms always seem to know what to say when you're sad.
Maybe not getting Rocket Guy wasn't that bad.

Alex did help that girl raise money for camp.
And he still had the money from Grandma and Gramps.

Alex got out his piggy bank and, unlike before,
he put *back* the five dollars that he took to the store.
Then he added three dollars as well as two dimes,
saving eight dollars and twenty cents for the next time.

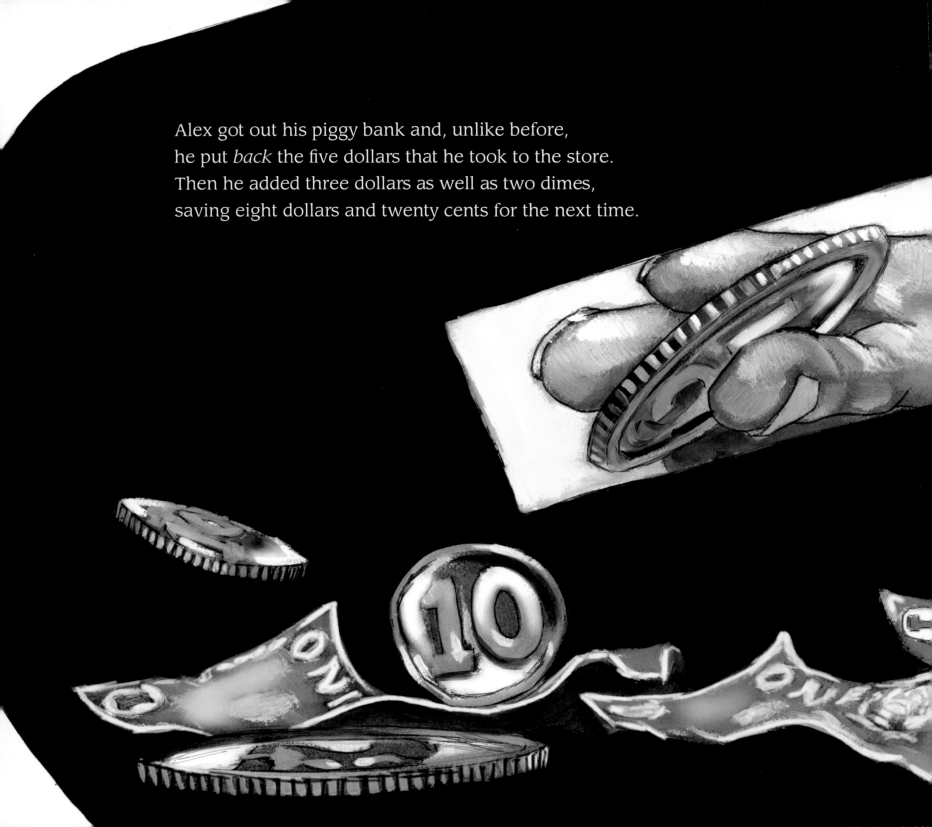

Sunday was his party with all of his friends.
They played games, ate cake and opened gifts at the end.
He was given puzzles and cars and toys for the yard.
Then his mom said,

"Son, did you see this card?"

Alex tore open the card
and read it aloud.
It said, *Happy Birthday, Son!*
You make us so proud!

He held out ten dollars from his mom and his dad.
"This birthday" said Alex, "is the best one I've had!"

"Now," said Mom, "You have
enough money to buy
that new toy you wanted.
What's his name? Rocket Guy?"

"I've changed my mind," said Alex.

"I've decided to wait."

"Saving your money?" said Mom.

"Well, isn't that great!"

"Mom," said Alex, "you know how you always say
that I should save my money for a rainy day?
Well, how about sunny days? Do they count too?"
"Of course," said Mom. "How you save is up to you!"

"I think I like saving for a sunny day best.
So I'll go get my bank and add this to the rest.
And on the next sunny day, when it gets really hot,
that lemonade and ice cream will sure hit the spot!"

Make Your Own Piggy Bank!

What you'll need:

- Empty plastic bottle (one-liter soda bottle or eight-ounce water bottle)
- 3-4 pieces of construction or scrapbooking paper
- 4 wooden beads or pom-poms
- 1 pipe cleaner
- Scissors
- Tape
- Glue
- A grown-up to help

Step 1:
Peel off the label from the bottle. Rinse the bottle with hot, soapy water and let it dry.

Step 2:
Cut a large strip out of the construction paper and wrap it around the bottle. Use tape or glue to hold the paper in place. Trace the bottle cap onto a piece of the same paper. Cut it out and glue it onto the cap of the bottle to make the snout.

Step 3:
Draw two big ear shapes on another piece of construction paper. They should look like rounded triangles. Then, draw two small inner ear shapes on another colored paper. Cut them out and then glue the smaller ear shapes onto the larger ones. Bend back the bottom part of the ear as a tab to glue onto the top of your bottle.

Step 4:
Cut out small circles for eyes and nostrils for the snout and glue those onto your bottle and bottle cap. Glue the pom-poms or beads onto the bottom for the piggy's feet.

Step 5:
Ask a grown-up to cut a slot at the top for coins; a utility knife works best. Next, have them cut a small hole in the back to insert the pipe cleaner and coil it like a tail.

Step 6:
Start saving!